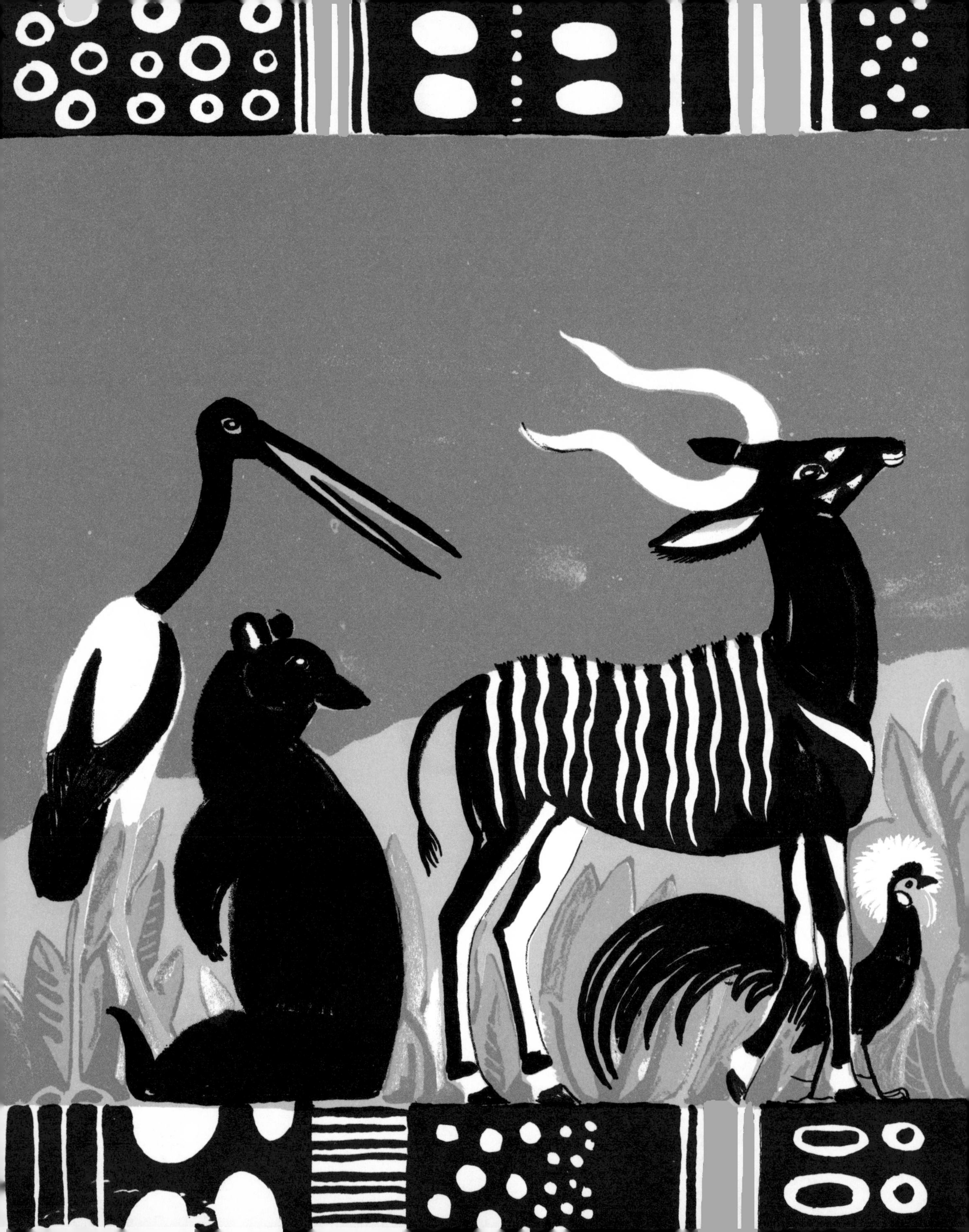

BLACK
and WHITE

DAHLOV IPCAR

Alex Spiro and Sam Arthur
would like to thank Robert Ipcar for his invaluable
assistance with this project and Dahlov Ipcar for her
beautiful words and pictures and for the honour
to introduce them to a new generation of children.

We would also like to thank the Nobrow design
team for their meticulous labour on the restoration
of the artwork to its original form.

This is a first Flying Eye Books edition.
Black and White is © 2015 Flying Eye Books.
First published as a Borzoi Book by Alfred A. Knopf, Inc. in 1963.

Published in the UK by Flying Eye Books, an imprint of Nobrow Ltd.
62 Great Eastern Street, London, EC2A 3QR.
ISBN 978-1-909263-63-5

Published in the US by Flying Eye Books, an imprint of Nobrow (US) Inc.,
611 Broadway, Suite #742, NY 10012, New York, USA
ISBN 978-1-909263-44-4

Order from www.flyingeyebooks.com

JUN 30 2015

for
Lilie Benbow
and Job

A little black dog and
a little white dog
were friends,

And they stayed together
and played together
all day long.

They played in the snow when the sun was bright.
They chased a cat that was snowy white.
They raced with a snow-white snowshoe hare,
and dug for a white rat that wasn't there,

Till the little white dog was lost from sight
Deep in a snow bank cold and white.
But he came back up –

          So that was all right.

They ran home late through the deepening night.
They found a small black-velvet mole
And sniffed at a black rat in his hole.
They barked and barked at a fluttering bat,
And the little black dog chased a coal-black cat,
Until they vanished out of sight
Far away in the pitch-black night.
But he came back again –

                      so that was all right.

The little black dog and the little white dog
Went in their houses and said good night.
They climbed in their beds and they curled up tight.

The night outside grew dark and deep,
And each dreamed a dream when he fell asleep.

The little black dog
all curled up tight
Dreamed a dream
of a jungle night.

In the dark jungle
of his dream
Big black elephants
ford a stream.

Black-and-white monkeys swing through trees,

While fierce black panthers sniff the breeze.

Black-and-white butterflies everywhere

Fill the flower-scented air.

Black-and-white zebras and antelopes graze

Through the long, hot jungle days.

While black-and-white birds
above them fly

Over the treetops
through the sky.

The little white dog
all snug and warm
Dreamed a dream
of an arctic storm.

In his dreamland's
ice and snow
Black-and-white seals
swim to and fro.

On the shore stand the polar bears,

While arctic foxes chase arctic hares.

Sea birds nest on the rocky shores

Where the big black walrus roars.

On his dream-sea tall ships sail,

And a great black whale meets a great white whale.

While through the swiftly flowing tide

Black-and-white fishes smoothly glide.

The little black dog and the little white dog
Woke again to a bright new day
And ran outside to race and play.
Two little puppy dogs, black and white,
Playing tag in the morning light.

And each one told the other his dream
Of the arctic storm and the jungle stream
And of all the animals black and white,
White as snow, black as night.